Tales from
AESOP

A Random House PICTUREBACK®

Tales from AESOP

by J.P. Miller

Random House
New York

9 0

The Hare and the Tortoise

The hare was making fun of the tortoise.

"What a slowpoke you are!" said the hare. "Your legs are so short I'm surprised that they ever get you anywhere. Just look at *my* long legs."

"Never you mind," replied the tortoise. "I can get around well enough. If you like, I'll race you to the pond."

The hare laughed at the idea of running a race with the tortoise, but for the sake of a good joke he agreed. The animals of the forest gathered to watch. They did not believe that the tortoise could ever beat the hare in a race.

When the hare and the tortoise were ready, the owl gave the starting signal by flapping his wings.

The hare, of course, quickly shot out of sight. But that did not bother the tortoise. He just went slowly and steadily on his way.

The tortoise continued to plod slowly and steadily down the road. He passed many of his friends. He even passed the sleeping hare.

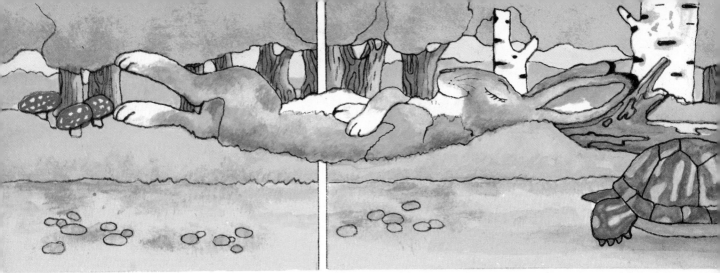

After running a short time, the hare grew tired. "I may as well rest awhile," he said. But before the hare knew it, he had fallen asleep.

But he never stopped—not even to get a cool drink. He just kept going down the hot, dusty road.

The hare did not wake up until the tortoise had almost reached the pond. He raced down the road as fast as his long legs would take him. But he was too late. The tortoise crossed the finish line before the hare could catch up.

*Slow and steady wins the race.

The Goose and the Golden Eggs

A farmer owned a gray goose that suddenly began to lay golden eggs. Every day, when he went to her nest, he found one solid-gold goose egg waiting for him.

In no time at all he became quite rich.

But soon one golden egg a day no longer satisfied the farmer.

"If I killed that goose and cut her open," he thought, "I could get all the gold at once. Then I would be the richest man in the country."

So he killed the goose and opened her up. But instead of finding a whole heap of golden eggs hidden inside, he found nothing at all.

*Take your good fortune as it comes.

The Dog and His Reflection

One day a dog stole a lamb chop from his master's table.

He rushed out of the house with it before anyone could stop him,
and never stopped running until he reached the woods.

As he carried the chop over a bridge, the dog looked down into the stream. There he saw his own reflection in the clear water. But he thought he was looking at another dog with another, bigger-looking lamb chop. Being greedy, he wanted to have *that,* too.

The dog let out a loud growl and opened his mouth to grab the other dog's chop. Alas! As soon as he opened his mouth, his own lamb chop dropped into the water and sank out of sight. Instead of having two chops, the greedy dog had nothing at all.

If you grab for more, you may lose what you already have.

The Shepherd Boy and the Wolf

A shepherd boy went out to the hills every day with his father's sheep. The pasture was a lonely spot beside a dark forest, and the hours passed slowly. The boy often longed for some company to make the time pass faster. He began to think it might even be fun if a wolf came to attack the sheep. Then everyone would come rushing, and there would be some excitement for a change.

One day the boy decided to give the alarm just to see what would happen. Hiding behind a tree, he shouted loudly, "Wolf! Wolf!"

The men in the village snatched up their clubs and guns and came running as fast as they could. But when they reached the pasture they saw no wolf. The sheep were grazing peacefully, and the shepherd boy was laughing.

"It was only a joke," he explained. "I wanted to see what would happen if I called for help."

Then one day a wolf really did creep into the pasture and fall upon the sheep. The frightened boy ran down the hill, screaming, "Wolf! Wolf!" as loudly as he could.

But the men in the village thought it was just another silly trick. They smiled at each other and shook their heads. They were not going to be fooled again.

So the wolf enjoyed himself, feasting upon the poor sheep.

When he finally vanished into the dark forest, the boy gathered what was left of his flock and returned to the village. He was sad and ashamed, but he had learned his lesson.

Those who lie are not believed when they finally tell the truth.

The Frog and the Ox

A big frog once lived in a small pond. Because he was the biggest creature in the pond, the frog decided he must also be the biggest thing in the world. As he sunned himself on his lily pad, he puffed out his chest with pride.

"No one anywhere is bigger than I am," he thought.

One day a huge ox came to drink at the pond. The frog was amazed, but he refused to be impressed.

"I suppose you think you are big," the frog called out to the ox. "But I want you to know that I can make myself just as big as you."

The ox did not reply. He just kept on drinking.

"If you don't believe me," shouted the frog, "just watch!"

The frog took a deep breath and blew himself up to twice his usual size. But still the ox paid no attention to him.

"So that's not big enough for you?" croaked the frog. "Very well, I'll make myself bigger still." He blew himself up even larger.

Again the ox said nothing. He simply turned away and headed for the other side of the pond. He had had enough to drink.

This made the frog furious. Taking an enormous breath, he blew . . . and blew . . . and blew himself up——

——until he burst. And that was the end of the big frog in the small pond.

*Don't try to be what you can't be.

The Farmer, the Son and the Donkey

A farmer and his son were driving their donkey to market, where they were going to sell him. They had not gone far when they met a troop of giggling girls.

"Look there!" cried one of them. "Aren't they a foolish pair to be trudging along on foot when one of them might be riding?"

When the farmer heard this, he told his son to get up on the donkey. And they went along happily until they came to a group of men talking by the side of the road.

"My, my!" said one of the men. "Just look at that young fellow riding in comfort while his poor old father has to walk."

"Get off that donkey, you lazy boy!" shouted another. "And let your father ride."

Right away the son slid off the donkey, and the farmer took his place. Before they had gone far, they passed a group of housewives.

"Why, you heartless old fellow!" cried several of the women at once. "How can you ride when your poor tired child can hardly keep up with you? What mean fathers there are nowadays!"

So the good-natured farmer pulled his son up behind him, and they both rode along on the donkey's back. When they reached the town, a villager pointed at them. "Tell me," he asked the farmer, "is that donkey yours?"

"Yes," replied the farmer.

"I would never have thought so," said the villager, "from the way you load him down. You should be ashamed! The two of you are better able to carry that poor beast than he is to carry you."

"You are right!" agreed the farmer. And he and his son got down from the donkey's back.

But how could they possibly carry the donkey? The farmer puzzled over this for a long time. Then at last an idea came to him. Cutting a thick branch from a nearby tree, he trimmed it into a stout pole. With some difficulty he and his son tied the donkey's feet to the pole and lifted both the pole and the donkey to their shoulders.

By the time they reached the town bridge, a whole crowd of people had gathered to hoot and laugh at the funny-looking sight. The donkey, frightened by the racket, took it into his head to kick at the ropes. All of a sudden he pulled loose from the pole and tumbled off the bridge into the water. Since he was unable to swim, he soon drowned.

The farmer and his son hung their heads in shame and started back home.

*If you try to please everyone, you may very well please no one at all.

The Crow and the Pitcher

A crow was about to die of thirst when he saw a pitcher of water standing on a stone wall.

Quickly the crow flew to the pitcher, thinking of the cool, refreshing drink he would have.

But his beak was not long enough to reach the water. The poor bird was not going to have his drink after all.

He flew to a tree stump. Just as the crow was about to give up, he spied some pebbles lying nearby.

Suddenly he had an idea! He flew over and picked up a pebble in his beak.

Carrying it in his beak, he dropped it into the pitcher. The level of the water rose just a little.

Then he brought another pebble and another. With each pebble, the water rose still higher.

By the time he had dropped all the pebbles into the pitcher, the water had reached the top. The clever crow then settled down beside the pitcher and drank his fill.

Never had any drink tasted so delicious.

If something seems impossible to obtain, try using your brain.